♥

This hothouse book belongs to

....

This edition published in 2013
Cottage Farm
NN6 0BJ

Text and illustrations © Sally Hunter, 2011

www.humphreys-corner.com

OCE001 0313
2 4 6 8 10 9 7 5 3

ISBN: 978-1-78197-134-5

Printed and manufactured in China

Humphrey's Playtime

Sally Hunter

Humphrey doesn't go to school yet so
he has lots of time to play!

He gets everything out of his box...

the train, blocks, boat, octopus,
caterpillar... and all the other toys.

other days Humphrey plays with his
special painted animals. "All aboard!
We are going on an adventure!"

"Come on Pinky up you go."

And sometimes Humphrey paints a lovely picture for Mommy. She especially likes rainbows and smiley sunshine faces.

"Da da da daaaa
...I'm a Superhero!"
shouts Humphrey.

He runs around
the house, jumps off
the chairs and makes
a lot of noise!

"Have you finished saving the world yet?"
asks mom.

Humphrey likes playing dress up in big shoes!

He walks about in them. Clomp Clomp!

Dad was late for work because his best shoes were in the toy box! oh Humphrey!

Henry Horse takes Humphrey on long journeys to different lands. It is all very exciting!

But they have to be back in time for dinner!

one time, Humphrey got lost at sea...
There were lots of monsters!
Good job Mop came to help.

Driving his little red car up and down the
hallway is one of Humphrey's best games...

but he sometimes bumps into mommy's legs!
oops Humphrey! Be careful!

"oh dear sounds like there is a problem. Don't worry, I will soon fix it

...and then it's time for a good wash!"

Humphrey has lots of fun in the yard too.
He has a look for George who lives next door...

makes roads for his cars and trucks...

And builds little houses out
of stones for the fairies.

In the yard, Humphrey has his very own swing.

"Hello Miss Birdy. How are you today?"

Humphrey has some creepy crawly friends too.
"Come on Simon, Sally and Sam Snail!
off we go! Choo Choo!"

Dad gets Humphrey's bike out of the garage.
"Look dad! Soon I can go on a big boy's bike!"

"Come on Mop, we are going for a ride.
Hold on tight!"

Humphrey has lots of lovely days,
playing in all these different ways...

But very best of all,
Humphrey likes...

looking after

cuddling...

SH

sharing with...

and Loving Mop.

His soft, floppy, one-eared little rabbit x